PUFFIN BOOKS

Margery Williams (1881–1944) was born in London but grew up in the United States of America, where she attended schools in Pennsylvania and Philadelphia. From 1925 she wrote under her married name, Margery Williams Bianco. She had one son and a daughter, Pamela Bianco, who went on to illustrate some of her mother's books. Williams wrote over twenty-five novels for adults and children, but she is best known for her timeless classic, *The Velveteen Rabbit*.

THE Velveteen RABBIT

MARGERY WILLIAMS

Illustrated by Justin Todd

PUFFIN

PUFFIN BOOKS

Published by the Penguin Group
Penguin Books Ltd, 80 Strand, London WC2R ORL, England
Penguin Group (USA) Inc., 375 Hudson Street, New York, New York 10014, USA
Penguin Group (Canada), 90 Eglinton Avenue East, Suite 700, Toronto, Ontario, Canada M4P 2Y3
(a division of Pearson Penguin Canada Inc.)
Penguin Ireland, 25 St Stephen's Green, Dublin 2, Ireland (a division of Penguin Books Ltd)
Penguin Group (Australia), 250 Camberwell Road, Camberwell, Victoria 3124, Australia
(a division of Pearson Australia Group Pty Ltd)
Penguin Books India Pvt Ltd, 11 Community Centre, Panchsheel Park, New Delhi – 110 017, India
Penguin Group (NZ), 67 Apollo Drive, Rosedale, North Shore 0632, New Zealand
(a division of Pearson New Zealand Ltd)
Penguin Books (South Africa) (Pty) Ltd, 24 Sturdee Avenue, Rosebank, Johannesburg 2196, South Africa

Penguin Books Ltd, Registered Offices: 80 Strand, London WC2R ORL, England

puffinbooks.com

First published by Heinemann in 1922
Published in Puffin Books 1995
17

Illustrations copyright © Justin Todd, 1995
All rights reserved

The moral right of the author and illustrator has been asserted

Set in Baskerville MT
Made and printed in England by Clays Ltd, St Ives plc

British Library Cataloguing in Publication Data
A CIP catalogue record for this book is available from the British Library

ISBN: 978-0-140-37335-6

THERE WAS ONCE A
velveteen rabbit, and
in the beginning he was
really splendid. He was
fat and bunchy, as a rabbit should
be; his coat was spotted brown and
white, he had real thread whiskers,
and his ears were lined with pink
satin. On Christmas morning, when
he sat wedged in the top of the
Boy's stocking, with a sprig of holly

between his paws, the effect was charming.

There were other things in the stocking, nuts and oranges and a toy engine, and chocolate almonds and a clockwork mouse, but the Rabbit was quite the best of all. For at least two hours the Boy loved him, and then Aunts and Uncles came to

dinner, and there was a great
rustling of parcels, and in the
excitement of looking at all the new
presents the Velveteen Rabbit was
forgotten.

For a long time he lived in the toy
cupboard or on the nursery floor,
and no one thought very much
about him. He was naturally shy,

and being only made of velveteen, some of the more expensive toys quite naturally snubbed him. The mechanical toys were very superior, and looked down upon everyone else; they were full of modern ideas, and pretended they were real. The model boat, who had lived through two seasons and lost most of his paint, caught the tone from them and never missed an opportunity of referring to his rigging in technical terms. The Rabbit could not claim to be a model of anything, for he didn't know that real rabbits existed; he thought they were all stuffed with sawdust like himself, and he understood that sawdust was quite out-of-date and should never be mentioned in modern circles. Even Timothy, the jointed wooden lion, who was made by the disabled soldiers, and should have had broader views, put on airs and pretended he was connected with Government. Between them all the poor little Rabbit was made to feel himself very insignificant and commonplace, and the only person who was kind to him at all was the Skin Horse.

The Skin Horse had lived longer

in the nursery than any of the
others. He was so old that his brown
coat was bald in patches and
showed the seams underneath, and
most of the hairs in his tail had
been pulled out to string bead
necklaces. He was wise, for he had

seen a long succession
of mechanical toys
arrive to boast and
swagger, and by-and-
by break their
mainsprings and pass
away, and he knew that
they were only toys, and
would never turn into
anything else. For nursery
magic is very strange and
wonderful, and only those playthings that are old and wise and
experienced like the Skin Horse
understand all about it.

"What is REAL?" asked the
Rabbit one day, when they were
lying side by side near the nursery
fender, before Nana came to tidy
the room. "Does it mean having

things that buzz inside you and a
stick-out handle?"

"Real isn't how you are made,"
said the Skin Horse. "It's a thing

that happens to you. When a child
loves you for a long, long time, not
just to play with, but REALLY
loves you, then you become Real."

"Does it hurt?" asked the Rabbit.

"Sometimes," said the Skin Horse,
for he was always truthful. "When

you are Real you don't mind being
hurt."

"Does it happen all at once, like
being wound up," he asked, "or bit
by bit?"

"It doesn't happen
all at once," said the Skin
Horse. "You become.
It takes a long time.
That's why it doesn't
often happen to people
who break easily, or have
sharp edges, or who have
to be carefully kept.
Generally, by the time
you are Real, most of
your hair has been
loved off, and your
eyes drop out and
you get loose in

the joints and very shabby. But these
things don't matter at all, because
once you are Real you can't be ugly,
except to people who don't
understand."

"I suppose you are Real?" said the
Rabbit. And then he wished he had
not said it, for he thought the Skin
Horse might be sensitive. But

the Skin Horse only smiled.

"The Boy's Uncle made me
Real," he said. "That was a great
many years ago; but once you are
Real you can't become unreal again.
It lasts for always."

The Rabbit sighed. He thought it
would be a long time before this
magic called Real happened to him.

He longed to become
Real, to know what it
felt like; and yet the
idea of growing
shabby and
losing his eyes and
whiskers was rather sad.
He wished that he could
become it without these
uncomfortable things
happening to him.

There was a person called Nana
who ruled the nursery. Sometimes
she took no notice of the playthings
lying about, and

sometimes, for no
reason whatever, she
went swooping about
like a great wind
and hustled them

away in cupboards. She called this
"tidying up", and the playthings all
hated it, especially the tin ones. The
Rabbit didn't mind it so much, for
wherever he was thrown he came
down soft.

One evening, when the Boy was
going to bed, he couldn't find the
china dog that always slept with
him. Nana was in a hurry, and it

was too much trouble to hunt for
china dogs at bedtime, so she simply
looked about her and, seeing that
the toy-cupboard door stood open,
she made a swoop.

"Here," she said, "take your old
Bunny! He'll do to sleep with you!"
And she dragged the Rabbit out by
one ear, and put him into the Boy's
arms.

That night, and for many nights
after, the Velveteen Rabbit slept in
the Boy's bed. At first he found it
rather uncomfortable, for
the Boy hugged him very
tight, and sometimes
he pushed him so
far under the
pillow that the
Rabbit could

scarcely breathe. And he missed,
too, those long moonlight hours in
the nursery, when all the house was
silent, and his talks with the Skin
Horse. But very soon he grew to like
it, for the Boy used to talk to him,
and made nice tunnels for him
under the bedclothes that he said
were like the burrows the real
rabbits lived in. And they had

splendid games together, in
whispers, when Nana had gone
away to her supper and left the
nightlight burning on the
mantelpiece. And when the Boy
dropped off to sleep, the Rabbit
would snuggle down close under his
little warm chin and dream, with
the Boy's hands clasped close round
him all night long.

And so time went on, and the little Rabbit was very happy – so happy that he never noticed how his beautiful velveteen fur was getting shabbier and shabbier, and his tail coming unsewn, and all the pink rubbed off his nose where the Boy had kissed him.

Spring came, and they had long days in the garden, for wherever the Boy went the Rabbit went too. He

had rides in the wheelbarrow, and picnics on the grass, and lovely fairy huts built for him under the raspberry canes behind the flower border. And once, when the Boy was called away suddenly to go out to tea, the Rabbit was left out on the lawn until long after dusk, and Nana had to come and look for him with the candle because the Boy couldn't go to sleep unless he was

there. He was wet through with dew and quite earthy from diving into the burrows the Boy had made for him in the flower-bed, and Nana grumbled as she rubbed him off with a corner of her apron.

"You must have your old

Bunny!" she said. "Fancy all that fuss for a toy!"

The Boy sat up in bed and stretched out his hands.

"Give me my Bunny!" he said. "You mustn't say that. He isn't a toy. He's REAL!"

When the little Rabbit heard that he was happy, for he knew that what the Skin Horse had said was true at last. The nursery

magic had happened to him, and he was a toy no longer. He was Real. The Boy himself had said it.

That night he was almost too happy to sleep, and so much love

stirred in his little sawdust heart
that it almost burst. And into his
boot-button eyes, that had long ago
lost their polish, there came a look
of wisdom and beauty, so that even
Nana noticed it next morning when

she picked him up, and said, "I
declare, if that old Bunny hasn't got
quite a knowing expression!"

That was a wonderful Summer!

Near the house where they lived

there was a wood, and in the long June evenings the Boy liked to go there after tea to play. He took the Velveteen Rabbit with him, and before he wandered off to pick flowers, or play at brigands among the trees, he always made the Rabbit a little nest somewhere among the bracken, where he would be quite cosy, for he was a kind-hearted little boy and he liked Bunny to be comfortable. One evening, while the Rabbit was lying there alone, watching the ants that ran to and fro between his velvet paws in the grass,

he saw two strange beings creep out
of the tall bracken near him.

They were rabbits like himself,
but quite furry and brand new.
They must have been very well
made, for their seams didn't
show at all, and they
changed shape in a queer way
when they moved; one minute they
were long and thin and the next

minute fat and bunchy, instead of
always staying the same like he did.
Their feet padded softly on the
ground, and they crept quite close
to him, twitching their noses, while
the Rabbit stared hard to see which
side the clockwork stuck out, for he
knew that people who jump
generally have something to wind
them up. But he couldn't see it. They

were evidently a new kind of rabbit altogether.

They stared at him, and the little Rabbit stared back. And all the time their noses twitched.

"Why don't you get up and play with us?" one of them asked.

"I don't feel like it," said the Rabbit, for he didn't want to explain that he had no clockwork.

"Ho!" said the furry rabbit. "It's as easy as anything." And he gave a big hop sideways and stood on his hind legs.

"I don't believe you can!" he said.

"I can!" said the little Rabbit. "I

can jump higher than anything!'' He
meant when the Boy threw him, but
of course he didn't say so.

"Can you hop on your hind legs?"
asked the furry rabbit.

That was a dreadful
question, for the
Velveteen Rabbit had
no hind legs at all!
The back of him

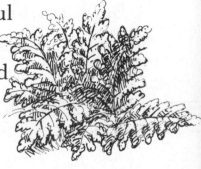

was made all in one piece, like a
pincushion. He sat still in the
bracken, and hoped that the other
rabbits wouldn't notice.

"I don't want to!" he said again.

But the wild rabbits have very
sharp eyes. And this one stretched
out his neck and looked.

"He hasn't got any hind legs!" he
called out. "Fancy a rabbit without

any hind legs!" And he began to laugh.

"I have!" cried the little Rabbit. "I have got hind legs! I am sitting on them!"

"Then stretch them out and show me, like this!" said the wild rabbit. And he began to whirl round and dance, till the little Rabbit got quite dizzy.

"I don't like dancing," he said. "I'd rather sit still!"

But all the while he was longing to dance, for a funny new tickly feeling ran through him, and he felt he would give anything in the world to be able to jump about like these rabbits did.

The strange rabbit stopped

dancing, and came quite close. He came so close this time that his long whiskers brushed the Velveteen Rabbit's ear, and then he wrinkled his nose suddenly and flattened his ears and jumped backwards.

"He doesn't smell right!" he exclaimed. "He isn't a rabbit at all! He isn't real!"

"I *am* Real!" said the little Rabbit. "I am Real! The Boy said so!" And he nearly began to cry.

Just then there was a sound of footsteps, and the Boy ran past near them, and with a stamp of feet and a flash of white tails the two strange rabbits disappeared.

"Come back and play with me!"

called the little Rabbit. "Oh, do come back! I *know* I am Real!"

But there was no answer, only the little ants ran to and fro, and the bracken swayed gently where the two strangers had passed. The Velveteen Rabbit was all alone.

"Oh, dear!" he thought. "Why did they run away like that? Why couldn't they stop and talk to me?"

For a long time he lay very still, watching the bracken, and hoping that they would come back. But they never returned, and presently the sun sank lower and the little Boy came and carried him home.

Weeks passed, and the little Rabbit grew very old and shabby,

but the Boy loved him just as much.
He loved him so hard that he loved
all his whiskers off, and the pink
lining to his ears turned grey, and
his brown spots faded. He even
began to lose his shape, and he
scarcely looked like a rabbit any
more, except to the Boy. To him he

was always beautiful, and that was
all that the little Rabbit cared
about. He didn't mind how he
looked to other people,
because the nursery
magic had made
him Real, and
when you are

Real shabbiness doesn't matter.

And then, one day, the Boy was ill.

His face grew very flushed, and he talked in his sleep, and his little body was so hot that it burned the Rabbit when he held him close. Strange people came and went in the nursery, and a light burned all night, and through it all the little Velveteen Rabbit lay there, hidden from sight under the bedclothes, and he never stirred, for he was afraid that if they found him someone might take him away, and he knew that the Boy needed him.

It was a long weary time, for the Boy was too ill to play, and the little Rabbit found it rather dull with

nothing to do all day long. But he
snuggled down patiently, and looked
forward to the time when the Boy
should be well again, and they
would go out in the garden amongst

the flowers and the butterflies and
play splendid games in the
raspberry thicket like they used to.
All sorts of delightful things he
planned, and while the Boy lay half

asleep he crept up close to the
pillow and whispered them in his
ear. And presently the fever turned,
and the Boy got better. He was able
to sit up in bed and look at picture

books, while the
little Rabbit
cuddled close at his
side. And one day,
they let him get up
and dress.

It was a bright,
sunny morning,
and the windows
stood wide open.
They had carried the Boy out on to
the balcony, wrapped in a shawl,
and the little Rabbit lay tangled up
among the bedclothes, thinking.

The Boy was going to the seaside

tomorrow. Everything was arranged,
and now it only remained to carry
out the doctor's orders. They talked
about it all, while the little Rabbit
lay under the bedclothes,
with just his head peeping
out, and listened. The
room was to be
disinfected, and all the
books and toys that the
Boy had played with in
bed must be burnt.

"Hurrah!" thought the
little Rabbit. "Tomorrow
we shall go to the
seaside!" For
the Boy had often
talked of the seaside,
and he wanted very
much to see the big

46

waves coming in, and the tiny crabs, and the sandcastles.

Just then Nana caught sight of him.

"How about his old Bunny?" she asked.

"*That?*" said the doctor. "Why, it's a mass of scarlet fever germs! —

Burn it at once.
What? Nonsense! Get
him a new one. He
mustn't have that any
more!"

And so the little
Rabbit was put into a
sack with the old picture-
books and a lot of rubbish,
and carried out to the end of the
garden behind the fowl-house. That
was a fine place to make a bonfire,
only the gardener was too busy just
then to attend to it. He had the
potatoes to dig and the green peas
to gather, but next morning he
promised to come quite early and
burn the whole lot.

That night the Boy slept in a
different bedroom, and he had a

new bunny to sleep with him. It was
a splendid bunny, all white plush
with real glass eyes, but the Boy was
too excited to care very much about
it. For tomorrow he was going to the
seaside, and that in itself was such a
wonderful thing that he could think
of nothing else.

And while the Boy was asleep,
dreaming of the seaside, the little

Rabbit lay among the old picture-
books in the corner behind the fowl-
house, and he felt very lonely. The
sack had been left untied, and so by
wriggling a bit he was able to get his
head through the opening and look
out. He was shivering a little, for he
had always been used to sleeping in
a proper bed, and by this time his
coat had worn so thin and

threadbare from hugging that it was no longer any protection to him. Nearby he could see the thicket of raspberry canes, growing tall and close like a tropical jungle, in whose shadow he had played with the Boy on bygone mornings. He thought of those long sunlit hours in the garden – how happy they were – and a great sadness came over him. He seemed to see them all pass before him, each more beautiful than the other, the fairy huts in the flower-bed, the quiet evenings in the wood when he lay in the bracken and the little ants ran over his paws; the wonderful day when he first knew that he was Real. He thought of the Skin Horse, so wise and gentle, and all that he had told him. Of what

use was it to be loved and lose one's
beauty and become Real if it all
ended like this? And a tear, a real
tear, trickled down his little shabby
velvet nose and fell to the ground.

And then a strange thing
happened. For where the tear had
fallen a flower grew out of the
ground, a mysterious flower, not at
all like any that grew in the garden.
It had slender green leaves the
colour of emeralds, and in the centre

of the leaves a blossom like a golden
cup. It was so beautiful that the little
Rabbit forgot to cry, and just lay
there watching it. And presently the
blossom opened, and out of it there
stepped a fairy.

She was quite the loveliest fairy in
the whole world. Her dress was of
pearl and dewdrops, and there were
flowers round her neck and in her
hair, and her face was like the most
perfect flower of all. And she came

close to the little Rabbit and gathered him up in her arms and kissed him on his velveteen nose that was all damp from crying.

"Little Rabbit," she said, "don't you know who I am?"

The Rabbit looked up at her, and it seemed to him that he had seen her face before, but he couldn't think where.

"I am the nursery magic Fairy," she said. "I take care of all the playthings that the children have loved. When they are old and worn out and the children don't need them any more, then I come and take them away with me and turn them into Real."

"Wasn't I Real before?" asked the little Rabbit.

"You were Real to the Boy," the Fairy said, "because he loved you. Now you shall be Real to everyone."

And she held the little Rabbit close in her arms and flew with him into the wood.

It was light now, for the moon had risen. All the forest was beautiful, and the fronds of the bracken shone like frosted silver. In the open glade between the tree trunks the wild rabbits danced with

their shadows on
the velvet grass, but
when they saw the Fairy
they all stopped dancing
and stood round in a ring to
stare at her.

"I've brought you a new
playfellow," the Fairy said.
"You must be very kind to him and
teach him all he needs to know in
Rabbitland, for he is going to live
with you for ever and ever!"

And she kissed the little Rabbit again and put him down on the grass.

"Run and play, little Rabbit!" she said.

But the little Rabbit sat quite still for a moment and never moved. For when he saw all the wild rabbits dancing around him he suddenly remembered about his hind legs, and he didn't want them to see that he was made all in one piece. He did not know that when the Fairy kissed him that last time she had changed him altogether. And he might have sat there a long time, too shy to move, if just then something hadn't tickled his nose, and before he

thought what he was doing he lifted his hind toe to scratch it. And he found that he actually had hind legs! Instead of dingy velveteen he had brown fur, soft and shiny, his ears twitched by themselves, and his whiskers were so long that they brushed the grass. He gave one leap and the joy of using those hind legs was so great that he went springing about the turf on them, jumping sideways and whirling round as the others did, and he grew so excited that when at last he did stop to look for the Fairy she had gone.

He was a Real Rabbit at last, at home with the other rabbits.

Autumn passed and Winter, and
in the Spring, when the days grew
warm and sunny, the Boy went out
to play in the wood behind the
house. And while he was playing,

two rabbits crept out from the
bracken and peeped at him. One of
them was brown all over, but the
other had strange markings under
his fur, as though long ago he had
been spotted, and the spots still

showed through.
And about his
little soft nose and
his round black
eyes there was
something
familiar, so that
the Boy thought to
himself:

"Why, he looks just like my old
Bunny that was lost when I had
scarlet fever!"

But he never knew that it really
was his own Bunny, come back to
look at the child who had first
helped him to be Real.